Dee Dee and Me

AMY SCHWARTZ

Holiday House / New York

For my mother

HOLIDAY HOUSE is registered in the U.S. Patent and Trademark Office.
Printed and Bound in April 2013 at Kwong Fat Offset Printing Co., Ltd., DongGuan City, China.
The text typeface is Agenda Light.
The artwork was created with gouache and pen and ink..
www.holidayhouse.com
First Edition
1 3 5 7 9 10 8 6 4 2
Library of Congress Cataloging-in-Publication Data
Schwartz, Amy.
Dee Dee and me / Amy Schwartz. — 1st ed.
p. cm.
Summary: Tired of the way she is treated by her big sister, Dee Dee,
and Dee Dee's friends, a little girl decides to leave home.
ISBN 978-0-8234-2524-2 (hardcover)
[1. Sisters—Fiction.] I. Title.
PZ7.S406Dee 2013
[E]—dc23
2012016565

Dee Dee is my sister.

She is five and a half inches taller than me.

Dee Dee says those five and a half inches
are where a person's brains are.

At breakfast, Dee Dee always asks me
if I want the second chocolate chip muffin.
Then she takes it.

Dee Dee said that my yellow apron with purple bows was the prettiest apron she'd ever seen.

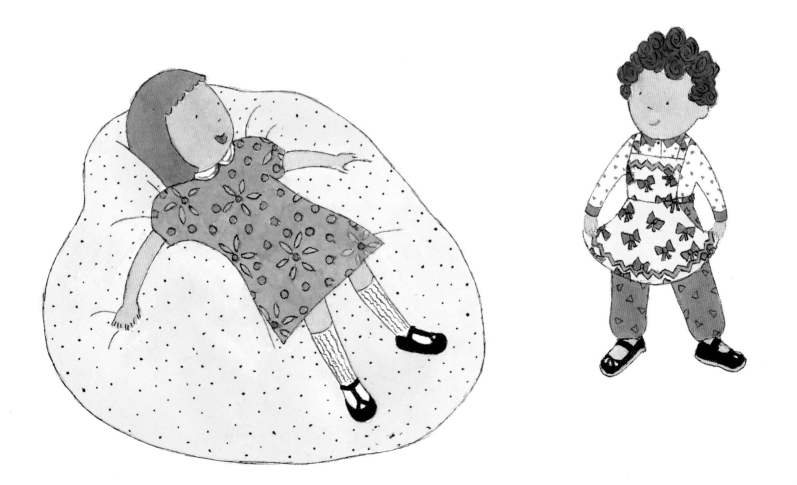

Then she cut it up to make a purse.

Dee Dee helped me catch my pet ladybug.
Then she shook the jar.

Dee Dee took Brown Bear
without asking.
She told me he looked funny
with only one eye.

When Dee Dee's friends Dinah
and Susie came to play,
Dee Dee said to me, "And Hannah,
 you can be the butler."

I made tiny cucumber sandwiches.
I served them on a fancy china plate.
Then Dee Dee said, "Butsy,
that will be all."

When my best friend,
Patsy, came over,
Dee Dee said,
"We'll play jacks."

Dee Dee hogged the ball.
She won every game.

We had a tea party.
Dee Dee was the Duchess.
She set the table, and she poured the tea.

We played dress up.

Dee Dee was the King, the Princess, and the Evil Queen.

When she left, Patsy said good-bye to Dee Dee and not to me.

The next time Patsy came over,
I told her I was too busy to
find Dee Dee.

When I got a new apron,
I told Dee Dee I was too busy
to show it to her.

On Saturday I told Dee Dee I was too busy
to have breakfast with her.

And I was.
I was packing my suitcase.
After I ran away from home,
I'd never have to see Dee Dee again.

I packed my new apron

and my birthday chocolate bar.

I packed my pet ladybug
in her jar.

Where was Brown Bear?
I couldn't find him.

I locked my suitcase.

After a snack I'd run away from home.

No more Dee Dee!

I put my hand on my head.

My brain was feeling bigger already.

I unlocked my suitcase
and ate my birthday chocolate bar.
I didn't have to share it with Dee Dee.
I licked my fingers.

I held my ladybug in a jar.
Nobody shook It.
She had beautiful spots.

Where was Brown Bear?
I checked under the bed.
He wasn't there.
I wanted Brown Bear!
I looked in the closet.
He wasn't there.

I put on my new apron.
I tied a double bow.
This apron would never be a purse!

Then I was the Evil Queen.

I pretended to be a Princess
in the mirror.
I put on my pearls and curtsied.

I had a tea party.
I poured the tea myself.
I was a very good Duchess.

I played jacks.
No one hogged the ball.
I won every game.

There was a knock on my door.
I opened it. It was Dee Dee.
She was holding Brown Bear.

"I sewed Brown Bear a new eye,"
Dee Dee said.
"Do you like it?"
"Yes," I said. "I do."

"Do you want to play dress up?"
Dee Dee asked.
I felt my head. My brain still felt big
"If when we have a tea party,
I can be the Duchess," I said.
"Okay," Dee Dee said.

"And if when we play dress up,
I can be the Evil Queen," I said.
"Okay," Dee Dee said.

"And if I want a snack," I said,
"you'll be Butsy."
"No," Dee Dee said. "I won't."

"Well I won't either," I said.
I retied my apron.
I put Brown Bear on the bed.

And then I played with Dee Dee.